BEAR'S SCHOO[L]
OSO EN LA ESCUELA

Written by • Escrito por Stella Blackstone

Illustrated by • Ilustrado por Debbie Harter

This is the school, where bears learn and play.
"Have fun!" wave the grown-ups. "You'll have a great day!"

Esta es la escuela, donde los osos aprenden y juegan.
—¡Que te diviertas! —dicen los adultos.
—¡Tendrás un gran día!

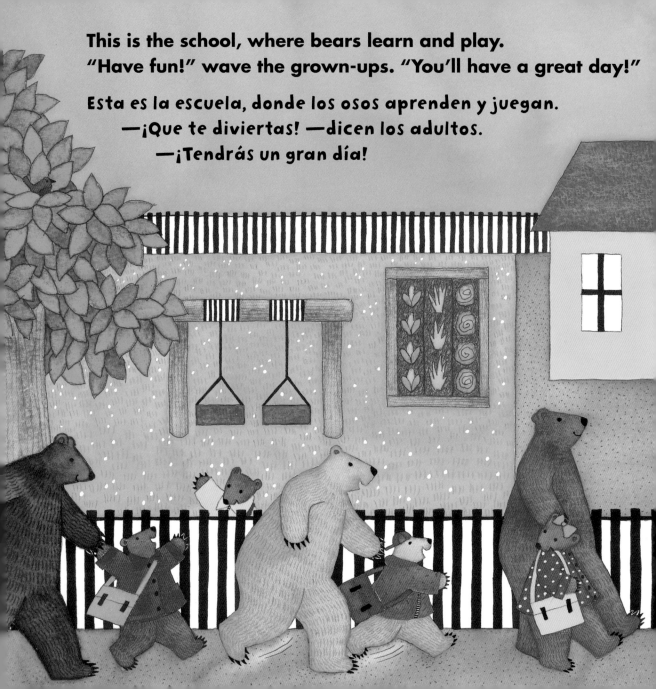

The school bell rings and the bears go inside.
They hang up their coats and their school bags with pride.

El timbre suena y los osos entran.
Todos cuelgan sus abrigos y mochilas con mucho satisfacción.

The first hour is spent learning music and sums.
Then the bears stop for a drink and a bun.

La primera hora la pasan aprendiendo música y sumas.
Después, los osos pausan para tomar y comer algo.

Next, the bears learn how to write out their names.
They sit with their friends and play some word games.

Luego, los osos aprenden a escribir sus nombres.
Se sientan con sus amigos y juegan algunos juegos de palabras.

It's already lunchtime! The hall is prepared
with tables and chairs for all of the bears.

¡Ya es hora de almorzar! El pasillo está preparado
con mesas y sillas para todos los osos.

After their meal, the bears have a rest.
They sleep for an hour, then wake up and stretch.

Después de su almuerzo, los osos descansan.
Duermen una hora, luego se despiertan y se estiran.

Hurray! It's playtime. The bears go outside.
They climb up the trees. They whoosh down the slide.

¡Bravo! Es hora de jugar. Los osos salen.
Suben a los árboles. Bajan por los toboganes.

Next, the bears make a newspaper giraffe.
Isn't she handsome? They all cheer and laugh.

Más tarde, los osos hacen una jirafa de papel periódico.
¿No es bonita? Todos se divierten y se ríen.

Storytime comes; the bears settle down
and hear about heroes of fame and renown.

Llega la hora de los cuentos. Los osos se sientan
y escuchan historias sobre héroes de fama y renombre.

The teacher steps out. The little bears follow.
"Goodbye, everybody! See you tomorrow."

El maestro sale del salón. Los ositos lo siguen.
—¡Adiós a todos! Nos vemos mañana.

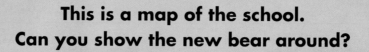

This is a map of the school.
Can you show the new bear around?

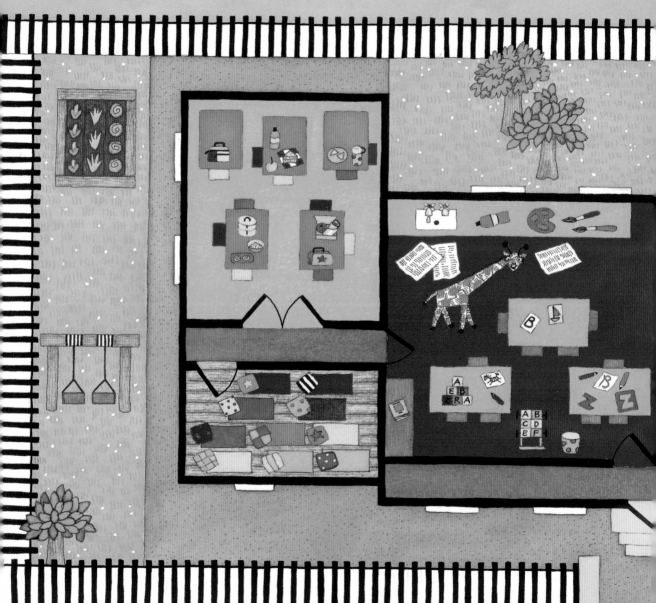

Este es un mapa de la escuela.
¿Puedes mostrarle la escuela al osito nuevo?

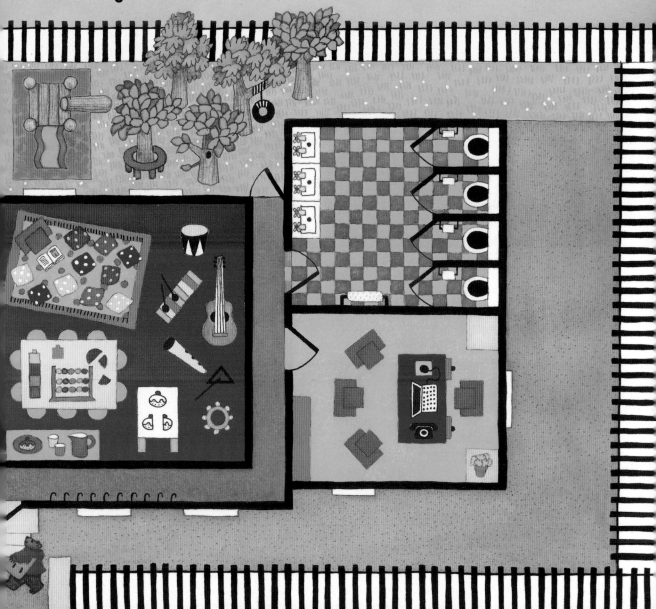

To the new Barefoot baby bears,
Milo, Lillian and Sasha, with love — S. B.
For Claire, Mike, Will and Ben — D. H. .

Barefoot Books
23 Bradford Street, 2nd Floor
Concord, MA 01742

Text copyright © 2014 by Stella Blackstone
Illustrations copyright © 2014 by Debbie Harter
The moral rights of Stella Blackstone and Debbie Harter have been asserted

First published in the United States of America by Barefoot Books, Inc in 2014
This bilingual Spanish paperback edition first published in 2022
All rights reserved

Graphic design by Judy Linard, London
Reproduction by B & P International, Hong Kong
Printed in China

This book was typeset in Slappy and Futura
The illustrations were prepared in paint, pen and ink, and crayon

ISBN 978-1-64686-689-2

Library of Congress Cataloging-in-Publication Data
is available under LCCN 2013029742

1 3 5 7 9 8 6 4 2